Secrets and Lies

Written by
Brian Keaney

Illustrated by Justine Dowling

CHAPTER ONE

After she had taken the register on Monday morning, Lauren's teacher, Ms Adams, looked up at the class and smiled. 'As you probably know,' she said, 'pupils from Year Five are going on a trip to Woolton Hall next weekend.'

The children nodded. They all knew about the trip to Woolton Hall nature centre and how much fun it was going to be. The Year Five pupils had been talking about nothing else for the last two weeks.

'Well, it turns out that there are some extra places on the trip,' Ms Adams continued, 'and we have decided to offer them to children from Year Four.'

Everyone in the class sat up when they heard this. Natasha's hand shot up.

'Miss, can I go?' she asked.

Ms Adams smiled and shook her head. 'I'm afraid that's not how we're going to do it, Natasha,' she said. 'We have to be fair. What I'm going to do is this. I've written everybody's name on a slip of paper and all the slips of paper have gone into this box.'

Lauren had been wondering what the box was doing on Ms Adams' desk. In fact she had been tempted to ask but now the explanation was clear. 'I'm going to put my hand into the box,' Ms Adams said, 'and pull out five names. Those five pupils will get the chance to go on the trip.'

Lauren considered what she knew about the trip to Woolton Hall. There would be forest walks, a trip to an old abandoned mine, a visit to some Roman remains and, of course, the children would be taking their sleeping bags and staying overnight. It sounded really good.

Ms Adams put her hand into the box and pulled out the first slip of paper. 'Daniel Murphy,' she announced. On the table next to Lauren, Daniel's face lit up. Ms Adams put her hand in again. 'Sharlene Akiri,' she read.

Sharlene looked all round the class, grinning. 'Natasha Davis,' Ms Adams

continued. Natasha punched the air. 'Yes!' she said.

With each announcement Lauren felt herself growing steadily more disappointed. She was certain now that she was not going to get picked. Ms Adams put her hand into the box for the fourth time. 'Zachary Marsden,' she said. Zach, who was sitting next to Daniel, looked astonished and delighted at the same time. Ms Adams put her hand into the box for the last time.

'And finally, Lauren Kirby,' she announced.

Lauren was so pleased she wanted to jump up and down and wave her hands in the air, but she didn't. Instead she just sat back in her chair with a contented smile and imagined what it was going to be like on the trip.

'I'm sorry you can't all go,' Ms Adams told the rest of the class, 'but of course you will have your turn next year. Natasha, Sharlene, Daniel, Zach and Lauren, I've got letters here for you to take home to your parents. You need to bring the signed permission slip back as soon as possible. Is that clear?'

'Yes, Miss,' all five of them chorused.

'Right,' Ms Adams said, 'I think that's enough about the trip. Now let's get down to some work.'

It isn't easy to work when you're excited, and Lauren kept thinking about the trip to Woolton Hall. The rest of the day seemed to take forever but at last the bell went for the end of school. Lauren got her coat and rushed outside to see her mother, who was standing talking to Daniel's mother. Lauren and Daniel lived in the same road so they usually walked back from school together.

Lauren went running up to her mother, brandishing the letter. 'Mum,' she said, 'I'm allowed on the trip to Woolton Hall.'

Her mother took the letter from Lauren. 'What's this?' she asked.

Daniel came up just then and held out his letter to his mother. 'It's a Year Five trip,' he said, 'but they had some extra places so some of us in Year Four are allowed to go with them.'

Lauren's mother was reading the letter now and for the first time that day a cold finger of doubt touched Lauren. Her mother was frowning. 'According to this letter you'd have to stay at the centre overnight,' she pointed out.

Lauren nodded. 'Everyone takes their sleeping bags,' she said. 'You sleep in dormitories.'

Lauren's mother continued to frown. Then she folded up the letter and put it in her bag. 'We'll talk about this later,' she said. 'But I can go, can't I?' Lauren asked her.

'We'll talk about it later,' her mother repeated.

Lauren didn't know what to say. She looked at Daniel and his mother, who were trying to pretend that nothing unusual had happened.

'Time we were going home,' her mother said. Reluctantly, Lauren followed her out of the school gates and down the road.

When they got home Lauren tried again. 'I can go on the trip, can't I?' she asked.

'I don't know, Lauren,' her mother said. 'I'll have to talk about it with your father.'

'The others are all going,' Lauren pointed out.

'I don't see how you can possibly know that, if they all got given the letters today,' her mother said. 'Besides, what other parents do is up to them. Your father and I have to make our own decisions about what we think is best for you.'

'Going on the trip is what's best for me,' Lauren insisted.

'That's enough, Lauren,' her mother said. 'I've told you. We'll talk about it later.'

There was nothing Lauren could do except wait for her father to come home. It wasn't fair. The other children would all be allowed to go, she was certain of that. Why did her mother and father have to be so strict?

As she asked herself this she glanced over at the photograph on the sideboard with the vase of flowers next to it. It was a picture of a little girl, just two years old. Her name was Ruth and she was smiling at the person who was holding the camera. She was Lauren's older sister, who had died of meningitis just a month after the

photograph had been taken. Lauren had been too young at the time to remember her sister, but she still sometimes found herself imagining what Ruth would have been like if she had lived.

Lauren's father came back at seven o'clock and she ran out to the hall to meet him. 'Dad,' she said, before he had taken off his coat, 'there's a school trip at the weekend and Ms Adams says there's a place for me and I have to get my parents' permission. I can go, can't I?'

'Lauren,' her mother said, coming along behind her, 'give your dad a chance to get his coat off before you start badgering him.'

Lauren waited patiently while her father hung his coat on the banister, went into the kitchen and sat down at the table. Then she started again. Her father listened carefully then he looked at her mother. 'Your mum and I will have to talk about it properly,' he said.

Lauren sighed. It was like banging her head against a brick wall.

That evening when she was getting into bed, she made one last attempt. 'Mum, have you and Dad talked about the trip?' she asked.

'Yes we have, Lauren,' her mother said gravely.

'And can I go?'

'We don't think it's a good idea, Lauren.'

Lauren felt her eyes filling up with tears. 'But why not?'

'Because this trip is really intended for older children and we don't like the idea of you spending the night away from home.'

'I'd be all right.'

'Maybe you would and maybe you wouldn't. Anyway, we've made up our minds now. I'm sorry if that's a disappointment to you but we have to do what we think is best.'

She bent over Lauren to kiss her on the cheek but Lauren turned her face away.

That night she dreamed about Ruth. In the dream she and Ruth were going on the trip together. They were talking about how much fun it would be. When she woke up she almost believed for a moment that it was real. Then she remembered the truth.

The next day Lauren told everyone at school that she was going to visit friends with her mum and dad on the weekend of the trip, so that meant she couldn't go. She didn't feel very comfortable lying like this but it was better than telling the truth.

Daniel, Zach, Natasha and Sharlene all got permission to go, just as Lauren had predicted, and they had a great time. In the playground the following Monday they told the rest of the class all about going down the coal mine.

'When we got underground, they turned off all the lights for a minute,' Daniel said.

Zach grinned. 'It was really scary,' he added.

'I wasn't scared,' Natasha said.

'Neither was I,' Sharlene agreed.

'Then why did you scream?' Daniel asked.

'I was laughing,' Sharlene told him.

Lauren didn't wait to hear any more. It only made her feel worse. She walked away to a corner of the playground where she could be by herself, and waited for the bell to ring.

CHAPTER TWO

A few weeks after the Woolton Hall trip Lauren was in the playground playing elastics with Natasha and Sharlene. Elastics was a game that had suddenly become a craze at their school. Two girls stood opposite each other with a length of elastic stretched around their ankles, making two long lines between them. Then a third girl had to jump so that her feet landed on either side of the two lines, in between the two lines and finally on top of the two lines, chanting, 'England, Ireland, Scotland, Wales, inside, outside, donkeys' tails.'

It was Lauren who was doing the jumping. She had just got to donkeys' tails for the second time when she saw Serena walking towards them.

Serena had joined their class at the beginning of term when her family had moved to England from Barbados. At the time Ms Adams had asked Lauren to help her settle in but in fact Serena didn't need much help settling in.

She was a confident girl with a friendly smile and a good sense of humour, and she quickly became very popular in the class.

Lauren saw that Serena was holding a little bundle of pink envelopes. She waited for the girls to stop playing, then she handed them one each.

'What's this?' Natasha asked.

Serena smiled. 'Invitations to my birthday party,' she said.

The three girls tore open the envelopes quickly and read their invitations. 'Serena Wallington invites you to her sleepover party on Friday 26th from six o'clock onwards.'

As soon as she read the word 'sleepover' Lauren knew there would be trouble with her parents. She glanced at Natasha and Sharlene. They were both smiling broadly.

'Are you all going to come?' Serena asked.

'Oh yes!' said Sharlene and Natasha together.

The three girls looked at Lauren, waiting for her to reply. 'Of course,' she said. 'I wouldn't miss it for the world.'

After school that day Lauren was walking home with Daniel as usual. They were a little way ahead of their mothers and their conversation could not be overheard, so Lauren took the opportunity to tell Daniel about the party.

'Serena's having a sleepover for her birthday,' she said.

'Yeah, I heard,' Daniel replied. He wasn't really very interested since it was an all-girls party.

'She gave me an invitation,' Lauren went on.

'Are you going?'

'I want to,' Lauren said, 'but I don't know whether my mum will let me.' She glanced over her shoulder to make sure that her mother wasn't listening.

'Why don't you just show your mum the invitation and see what she says?' Daniel suggested.

Lauren looked unhappy. 'Because she might say I can't go and what am I going to do then?' she asked him.

Daniel shrugged. 'You could try to explain that you really want to go,' he said.

Lauren sighed. She couldn't see that working. They had reached Lauren's house by now and a moment later their mothers drew level with them. 'Come on now,' Daniel's mum said, 'I've got a lot of things to do when we get back.'

They said goodbye and Lauren followed her mother indoors. It was no good talking about it with Daniel. He didn't understand. The trouble was, nobody understood.

CHAPTER THREE

After he'd got home from school, put away his school stuff and had something to eat, Daniel went round to see Zach. Zach's eyes had a special gleam in them when he opened the door. 'You wait until you see this new computer game that Edward's got,' he said as he led the way upstairs. 'It's called Zombie Warriors and it's really good. You have this army of warriors and you have to fight against these other armies of vampires, werewolves and wraiths.'

Zach pushed open the door to Edward's room and they stood for a moment looking in. It was a bit of a mess. The curtains weren't drawn and the bed wasn't made, and there were clothes and books all over the floor.

'Won't Edward mind us playing his game?' Daniel asked.

'He's gone out,' Zach said, going over to the computer on the desk against the wall and turning it on. 'He won't know anything about it.'

Daniel was still standing in the doorway, hesitating. 'What if he comes back while we're playing the game?' he asked.

'Don't worry. He won't be back for ages,' Zach said. 'He's gone bowling. There's this girl he's interested in called Charmaine and he thinks she's going to be at the bowling alley this evening.'

'And will she?' Daniel asked.

'Who cares?' Zach said. 'Come on, let me show you what this game is like.'

Soon the two of them were engrossed in fighting werewolves, vampires and wraiths.

They didn't notice the time passing and a whole hour went by as warriors battled against each other. Downstairs, the front door opened, Edward came inside and went straight upstairs to his room. He stopped in his tracks when he found Zach and Daniel sitting at his computer, playing his game. 'What are you two doing in my room?' he demanded. 'And who said you could use my computer?'

Zach and Daniel were taken by surprise. They jumped to their feet. 'Sorry, Edward,' Zach said. 'I thought you wouldn't mind us playing because you weren't here.'

'You thought I wouldn't mind!' Edward looked as though he could hardly believe his ears. 'Well you were wrong, because I do mind. I mind very much.' He strode across the room, turned off the game and took the disk out of the computer. 'Don't you dare touch my stuff!' he told Zach.

'All right,' Zach told him. 'I said I'm sorry.'

'You will be sorry if it ever happens again,' Edward said. He gave Zach a shove that made him stagger backwards. 'Do you understand what I'm saying?' he demanded.

'Yes, I understand,' Zach said. 'I'm sorry I touched your stupid game.'

Then he and Daniel went out of the room as quickly as they could.

They went and sat in Zach's room and Zach showed Daniel his latest superhero models. He was collecting the whole set, but neither of the two boys could really summon up much enthusiasm for them.

'Edward was in a bad mood,' Daniel said.

'He's always in a bad mood. He gets on my nerves. He thinks he's so cool and he's not. He's just a stupid idiot. One of these days I'm going to get my own back on him,' muttered Zach.

The two boys sat there for a little while longer without speaking. Daniel couldn't really see how Zach was ever going to get his own back on Edward but he didn't say so.

CHAPTER FOUR

Lauren's mother was in the kitchen chopping an onion for dinner. Lauren got herself a drink of squash from the refrigerator. Then she stood watching her mother for a little while, trying to pluck up the courage to say what was on her mind. She could feel Serena's invitation burning a hole in her pocket but she wasn't going to take it out and hand it over to her mother. Not just yet. She needed to approach this carefully. 'Mum?' she began.

'Yes?' her mother said, still chopping the onion.

'What do you think about sleepovers?'

'I don't know what you mean.'

'You know, a party where you stay the night.'

Her mother finished chopping the onion and put it into the frying pan. She added some oil and turned on the gas. 'I don't know,' she said. 'It sounds like a silly idea to me.'

That didn't sound very hopeful. Lauren tried a different approach.

'What age do you think someone should be allowed to go to a sleepover?' she asked.

Her mother frowned. 'I really don't know. Why are you asking these questions?'

'Oh, I just wondered.'

'Well, much older than eight anyway,' her mother said.

Lauren's heart sank. 'Do you really think so?' she asked.

'Yes,' her mother said firmly. 'Now I've got a lot to do in here, Lauren, so why don't you go and see if there's anything you'd like to watch on the television?'

'Yes, Mum,' Lauren said miserably.

That evening Lauren tried talking to her dad. He was sitting on the sofa watching the television. 'Dad, what age do you think a girl should be allowed to go to a sleepover?' she asked him.

'What?' he said, without looking up from the TV screen.

'What age do you think a girl should be allowed to go to a sleepover?' she repeated.

He turned down the volume. 'What's a sleepover?'

She told him.

He thought about it. 'I don't know,' he said after a moment. 'Have you asked your mum?'

'Yes.'

'What did she say?'

'She said much older than eight.'

'Well there you are then.'

'But what do you think?'

'I agree with your mum.' He turned the volume back up again.

Lauren gave up and went out of the room. She went upstairs to her bedroom and sat on the bed feeling miserable.

She glanced up at the collection of soft toys and teddy bears that stared down at her from the top shelf. She hadn't played with any of them for years but she felt a sudden urge to get them all down and cuddle them.

That night, as she lay in bed, Lauren thought to herself. Tomorrow I'm going to show Mum the invitation and explain that I really have to go, and she's going to listen and then she's going to say, 'All right then, Lauren, since the other girls are going, I suppose you'd better go too.' She felt better for telling herself this. Then she closed her eyes and went to sleep.

But when she woke up the next day it didn't seem quite so easy to talk about the party. Several times that morning she nearly took the invitation out of her pocket and showed it to her mother, but each time her mother said something that made Lauren realise that it was not the best time to try her luck.

She made up her mind that she would definitely talk about it in the afternoon, but when she had finally plucked up the courage to speak, her mother said, 'Lauren, you've got your piano lesson in half an hour. You'd better do some practice.' So that was another opportunity wasted.

That night as Lauren lay in bed, with the soft toys still looking down at her from the top shelf, she told herself that on Sunday she would show her mother the invitation whatever happened.

But on Sunday it was just the same. Every time Lauren plucked up the courage to try and talk about the party something would happen to stop her. And by bedtime Lauren had still not shown her mother the invitation.

Every morning of the following week, as soon as she woke up, Lauren would decide that today was going to be the day she would tell her mother about the invitation. But every night she went to sleep without doing so. Her friends at school were talking about what they had bought Serena for a present and what they were going to wear for the party, but Lauren could only listen and try to smile.

On Thursday during the Numeracy Hour, when Lauren was working in a group with Natasha and Sharlene, Natasha said, 'So what have you bought for Serena?'

Lauren didn't know what to say. She could feel herself blushing. Finally she said, 'It's a secret.'

'Are you sure you really have bought a present?' Natasha asked.

'Can you girls please stop talking and get on with your work,' Ms Adams said crossly. For the first time in her life Lauren felt pleased to be told off by her teacher.

CHAPTER FIVE

At last the day of the party arrived. Of course not everyone in the class was thinking about it. Zach and Daniel were standing in the playground talking about Zombie Warriors. 'I wish we could play it tonight,' Daniel said.

'So do I,' Zach replied. 'Edward's going out tonight as well, so it wouldn't make any difference to him.'

'Where's he going?' Daniel asked.

'He's finally got a date with that girl, Charmaine,' Zach said. 'He rang her up and asked her to go to the cinema with him, and she said yes. You should have seen him afterwards. He was so pleased with himself. Do you know who she is?' asked Zach.

'How should I know?'

'She's Serena's big sister.'

'Serena in our class?'

'Do you know any other Serenas?'

Daniel had to admit that he didn't.

'He's not going out until late, worse luck,' Zach said. 'Otherwise we could sneak in and play it. But it's not worth the risk. I'd be in big trouble if he found me in his room again.'

In another part of the playground Lauren was watching Natasha and Sharlene walk towards her. They were both smiling but there was something about those smiles that Lauren didn't like. She felt like a mouse, trapped by a pair of cats.

'Hi, Lauren,' Natasha said. 'All ready for the party tonight?'

'You bet,' Lauren said.

The two girls looked meaningfully at each other. 'You are coming, aren't you?' Natasha asked.

'Of course I'm coming,' Lauren said, and she tried to sound as though she believed it.

'We thought maybe you weren't allowed,' Sharlene said.

'Of course I'm allowed,' Lauren told them. She could see Natasha raising her eyebrows. 'I'm going to get a drink of water,' she said, quickly walking away. As she went, she was sure she could hear them giggling.

That evening she was walking home with Daniel as usual, and they were talking about what had happened during the day at school. Someone had put chewing gum in Emma Wilkinson's hair. Ms Adams was furious. She had stood in front of the class and demanded to know who was responsible. But no one had owned up and the whole class had been kept in at lunchtime.

'Who did put it there?' Daniel asked.

'I think it was Natasha,' Lauren said.

'She would,' Daniel said. He took a packet of sweets out of his pocket and offered one to Lauren.

'Thanks,' she said, popping it into her mouth.

'Have you given your mum the invitation yet?' Daniel asked.

She shook her head. 'Not yet.'

'Why not?'

'Because I'm scared.'

'What are you scared of?'

'That she won't let me go.'

'But the party's tonight, isn't it?'

'Yeah.'

'So what are you going to do if she doesn't let you go?'

'She's just got to,' Lauren said. 'If she doesn't, I'll …' She struggled to think of what she would do. 'I'll go anyway,' she said at last.

'Will you really?' Daniel asked.

'Yes really!' she said.

Daniel looked as though he didn't believe her.

'I mean it!' she told him.

They had arrived outside Lauren's house by now and their mothers were saying goodbye. 'You won't tell anyone what I said will you?' Lauren whispered. 'Of course I won't,' Daniel whispered back.

'Promise?'

'If you like,' Daniel said. 'Who's going to ask me anyway?'

When they got inside, Lauren knew that this was her last chance to tell her mother about the party. So as soon as they had both taken off their coats, she began, 'Mum, there's this girl at school called Serena.'

But her mother interrupted her. 'Lauren, would you mind telling me this some other time,' she said. 'I've got a terrible headache, I think I might go and lie down upstairs for a while.'

'But, Mum, I just wanted to tell you something.'

'Not now, darling. Tell me later.'

Her last hope was gone. Lauren stood there feeling utterly miserable, watching her mother retreating upstairs. Then she went into the front room and sat on the sofa staring at the television and thinking about how the other girls would be getting ready for the party right now.

It was going to be so much fun, probably the best party that anyone had been to, and she was going to miss it. She was like Cinderella, not allowed to go to the ball, except that unlike Cinderella, she didn't have a fairy godmother. She felt so miserable she was just about ready to burst into tears. Then a thought came to her. What if she became her own fairy godmother?

She looked at her watch. Her father

would not be home until seven o'clock. She could leave before he arrived. Of course her mum and dad would be worried when they found that she was gone, but she could leave them a note so they'd know she was all right. And once she was gone they wouldn't be able to do anything about it.

The more she thought about it, the more she wanted to do it. Her mum and dad would be angry but when they saw that she was okay and that she could look after herself, well they'd probably be pleased. Yes, that was what she would do, her mind was made up. She stood up, tiptoed upstairs to her room and began to get ready for the party. She changed into her best clothes and packed an overnight bag.

She realised she needed some money for the bus. When Serena had been talking about the party at school she had told them which bus went down her road. Lauren had been pleased because the same bus stopped not far from her house. She opened her money box. There was some money inside that she had been given for her birthday. She took out two pound coins. Then all she had to do was write the note for her parents.

She had a bit of difficulty trying to decide what to say in the note. In the end she just wrote,

Dear Mum and Dad,
I'm staying the night with a friend. Don't worry about me.

Love,
Lauren
x

She put it on her bed where it could easily be found. She looked at her watch. It was a quarter to six. She opened the door of her bedroom and quietly stepped outside on to the landing. She paused outside her mother's room, listening carefully, but there was no sound. She crept downstairs, being careful not to make any noise, went down the hall and opened the front door very quietly. She stepped outside and shut the door softly behind her.

CHAPTER SIX

It was dark outside and as Lauren closed the front gate behind her she felt scared. She turned and looked back at her house. It still wasn't too late to turn back but she thought of what the other girls would say if she didn't arrive at the party, and instead she made her way quickly to the bus stop.

She didn't have to wait long before a bus came along. She asked the bus driver how many stops it was to Serena's road. He gave her a long look and she thought at first he was going to ask her what she was doing out on her own so late, but in the end he told her that it was six stops, took her money and gave her a ticket.

There weren't many passengers on the bus; a middle-aged woman carrying a bag of shopping seemed to be watching her as she found a seat by herself, but, like the bus driver, the woman said nothing.

The window beside her was all steamed up so Lauren rubbed it clear with her sleeve and looked out as the bus pulled away.

It was strange being on the bus on her own and Lauren couldn't help feeling a little frightened. She kept glancing at the other passengers, worried that they were watching her. The expressions

on their faces all seemed disapproving. An elderly couple just behind her were looking in her direction and talking quietly to themselves. She felt sure they were discussing her. She concentrated on counting the stops. Whatever else happened she had to get off at the right place.

The bus seemed to go incredibly slowly. Every traffic light seemed to be stuck at red, and Lauren was sure that someone would come up to her before she reached her stop and demand to know whether her parents knew where she was. But no one did and at last it was her stop.

Gratefully she stepped down from the bus, looked about her and saw a road sign. Sure enough, she was on Serena's road. She felt pleased with herself then. She could manage perfectly well on her own. She walked along the street, checking the numbers until she found the right one.

She had butterflies in her stomach as she rang the front doorbell. Serena's mother looked a bit surprised when she opened the door and found Lauren on her own. 'Did you come by yourself?' she asked, looking around for Lauren's mum or dad.

Lauren shook her head. 'My parents dropped me off at the door,' she said quickly.

'You'd better come in then,' Serena's mother replied.

As soon as Lauren stepped inside Serena's house and saw the little piles of wrapping paper on the floor of the sitting room and the collection of cards arranged on the mantlepiece, she realised that she had forgotten all about a present for Serena. She had been so busy worrying about whether she would be allowed to go to the party that everything else had slipped her mind. The other girls were all looking intently at her.

'Oh, Serena,' she said. 'I'm so sorry – I forgot your present and your card.'

Serena looked disappointed, and
Lauren stood there feeling awkward and
wishing she had not come to the party
after all.

It was Serena's mother who smoothed
things over. 'Never mind,' she said. 'You
can give them to Serena when you see
her next. Now why don't you take off
your coat and join in the party?'
Gratefully, Lauren did as Serena's
mother had suggested.

'We're going to watch videos in my
bedroom,' Serena said then, and the girls

all followed her upstairs to see what videos her mother had rented for them. In a little while the business of the present was forgotten, and Lauren found she was beginning to relax and enjoy herself.

While Lauren and her friends were looking through the videotapes, Daniel and his parents had some visitors – Lauren's mother and father.

Daniel could tell right away that something was wrong. Lauren's mother's face was blotchy, as though she had been crying. Her father was looking grim-faced. It didn't take very long before he found out what had happened. Lauren's mother explained how they had discovered that Lauren had gone missing, leaving a note saying she was staying the night with a friend. Daniel's mother looked at him. 'Do you know where she could be, Daniel?'

Daniel shook his head.

'Are you sure?' Lauren's mother asked.

Everyone was looking at Daniel and he was beginning to feel terribly uncomfortable.

'How should I know where she is?' he asked.

Lauren's mother sighed. 'I don't know what I'm going to do,' she said. 'It looks like I'm going to have to call the police.'

'I think you should try not to panic,' Daniel's mother said. 'Why don't you sit down for a moment and try to think where she might be.'

'I can't sit down,' Lauren's mother said. 'I'm so worried. What on earth has made her do this?' As she was saying this the tears were rolling down her cheeks.

Daniel looked on in dismay. He had never seen an adult crying before.

He took the opportunity to slip out of the room. He had a terrible feeling that he knew perfectly well where Lauren was and that he really ought to say, but he had promised Lauren that he would not reveal to anyone else what she had said to him. It was a terrible dilemma. He wished he could tell Lauren what was happening and make her realise the difficult position she had put him in. If only he could phone her and speak to her, but he didn't even know Serena's phone number. The Wallingtons hadn't been in the area long enough to be in the phone book.

Then he had an idea. He suddenly remembered what Zach had told him about Edward phoning up Charmaine, Serena's sister, and asking her for a date. That meant that Edward must know Serena's number. Quickly, Daniel went upstairs, picked up the phone in his parents' room and called Zach.

CHAPTER SEVEN

Zach was sitting at the kitchen table covering his exercise book for school. He had used pale blue paper and drawn Zombie Warriors all over it. Now all he needed was a label to put on the front. He remembered that he had a roll of sticky labels in his bedroom and went upstairs to get them.

He was halfway up the stairs when the telephone rang. Immediately Edward came out of the bathroom and pushed past Zach. 'Out of the way,' he said. 'That's for me.'

Zach sighed and went into his room. He had just found the sticky labels and put them in his pocket when his mother called up the stairs that the phone call was for him, not Edward. Zach went down and picked up the receiver.

It was Daniel of course. 'Listen, Zach, I need your help fast,' he said.

'What's the problem?' Zach asked.

Daniel explained about Lauren and the party.

'You mean she didn't tell her mum and dad she was going?' Zach said.

'That's right.'

'That's crazy.'

'I think she was frightened they wouldn't let her go.'

'But what's it got to do with me?' Zach asked.

Daniel explained about the promise he had made to Lauren. 'That's why I need to speak to her,' he went on, 'before her mum and dad ask me where she is.'

'But I don't see how I can help,' Zach said.

'All I need is the phone number of Serena's house,' Daniel told him, 'and Edward must have that because you said he rang up Charmaine to ask her for a date.'

Zach didn't like the sound of this. 'Edward's not going to give me his girlfriend's phone number,' he said. 'You know what he's like.'

'Couldn't you get it anyway?' Daniel asked. 'Without telling him, I mean.'

Zach couldn't believe what he was hearing. 'You want me to get the phone number without telling Edward?' he said. 'Are you crazy? I'd have to go into his room and snoop about, and if he caught me, he'd probably kill me.'

'I know it's a lot to ask,' Daniel said.

'A lot to ask! That's putting it mildly. Edward's in the house right now. He's in the bathroom getting ready for the date.'

'Okay,' Daniel said. 'I suppose you're right. I'd be too frightened to do it if he was my brother.'

'I didn't say I was too frightened,' Zach said.

'Didn't you?'

'Of course not! I'm not frightened.'

'Then you'll do it?'

Zach hesitated. 'I might.'

'That's great, Zach. Thanks a million.'

'That's okay.'

'Ring me back when you've got the number, will you?'

'Sure.'

After Zach had put the phone down he wasn't exactly sure why he had just agreed to Daniel's request, but now that he had said he would do it, he had to go through with it. So, taking a pencil and a sheet of paper from the message pad next to the telephone, he went very quietly upstairs, pausing outside the bathroom and listening. Sure enough Edward was in there. Zach could hear him brushing his teeth. Swiftly, Zach crossed the landing until he was standing outside Edward's room. He paused for a moment to summon up his courage. Then he opened the door and stepped inside.

Edward's room was a mess, like it always was. There were clothes all over the bed and on the floor, along with magazines, CDs, an empty drink can, a slice of toast and a pair of muddy football boots. What he needed to find was Edward's diary, but it wasn't easy to know where to begin looking.

He started by rummaging around on the floor. When he found nothing there he looked on Edward's desk, also without success. Then he saw Edward's school

bag beside the desk. Of course! That was where it would be. He grabbed the bag and began looking through its contents, but there was no sign of the diary. It had to be in the room somewhere, Zach told himself. He just needed to look more carefully.

He had just begun going through the bag for a second time when he heard the sound he had been dreading: the bathroom door opening and Edward's footsteps coming along the landing. Frantically, he looked towards the door but it was too late to escape now. He was trapped. He didn't have much time to think. Edward would be coming through the door at any moment. Quickly, he scrambled under the bed and held his breath, just as the bedroom door opened.

The first thing Zach saw as he got under the bed was a small black book with the word 'diary' written in gold letters, stuck between the mattress and the bed springs. So that was where he hid it!

Meanwhile, Edward was getting his jacket out of the wardrobe. From his position under the bed Zach watched as his brother put the jacket on and spent a long time looking at himself in the mirror. First he looked at himself from the front, then standing to one side and finally standing to the other side. Then he took the jacket off again, put it down on the bed and went downstairs.

Zach waited until he was absolutely sure that Edward had gone. Then he got out from under the bed, lifted up the corner of the mattress and took out the diary. He leafed through the pages and there it was: Charmaine's name and telephone number. He wrote it down on the piece of paper he had brought with him, then put the diary back in place. He put the piece of paper in his pocket. As he did so he felt something else in his pocket. He took it out and looked at it. It was the roll of sticky labels he was going to use for the cover of his exercise book.

Suddenly Zach had an idea. It was a dangerous idea, more dangerous even than being in Edward's bedroom, but it was a brilliant idea as well. He thought of the trouble he could get into if he went through with it, but he also thought of how glorious it would be if the idea worked! He made up his mind. He would give it a try.

On one of the sticky labels he wrote the words, 'I think I'm so cool'. Then he peeled it off the roll, stuck it on the back of Edward's jacket and turned the jacket over so that the label could not be seen. Then he got out of the room as quickly as he could, went downstairs and rang Daniel back with Serena's phone number.

CHAPTER EIGHT

Lauren was enjoying the party. The food had been terrific. Now the girls were drinking squash and watching a really good video when suddenly the bedroom door opened and Serena's mum appeared. She looked slightly puzzled. 'Lauren,' she said, 'there's someone on the phone for you.'

All the girls looked at Lauren and she felt herself blushing. 'Is it my mum?' she stammered.

Serena's mother shook her head. 'It's a boy,' she said.

'Lauren's got a boyfriend,' Natasha exclaimed.

Everybody went, 'Oooh!' and giggled, all except Lauren. She was confused. She couldn't think who it could be, but the only thing she could do was get up and follow Serena's mother downstairs. They went into the kitchen where Serena's mother handed her the receiver and walked away, though not far enough to be completely out of earshot.

Lauren put the telephone to her ear. 'Hello?' she said.

It was Daniel of course. 'Lauren, your parents are in my house,' he told her.

'Oh no!' she said. 'They can't be!'

'They are! They're downstairs and they want to know where you are. They're really worried and your mum is talking about phoning the police.'

Lauren stood there in a daze, listening to what Daniel was telling her. She simply didn't know what to say in reply.

'You've got to phone them and tell them where you are. Otherwise they're going to ask me and I'll have to tell them. Lauren, are you listening to me?'

Lauren was almost too frightened to speak. The police! That would be terrible. Of course she had known all the time that what she was doing was wrong but she had tried not to think about what would happen as a result. She had certainly never thought the police might be involved.

'Lauren, I can hear my mum calling

me,' Daniel said. 'I'm going to have to go downstairs in a minute. You must phone your mum and dad. Do you understand?'

'Yes,' Lauren said, but she spoke like somebody in a dream. 'I understand.'

Daniel hung up.

Lauren stood there, still holding the receiver in her hand, unable to move. In her heart she knew that Daniel was right – she ought to phone her mum and dad, but it was as though she had been turned into stone.

At last Serena's mother came over to her. 'Is something the matter?' she asked.

Lauren nodded slowly. She put down the receiver and turned to look at Serena's mother. She opened her mouth to say something but she found it difficult to speak because she was so near to tears.

'What's the matter then?' Serena's mother asked. She crouched down and took Lauren's hands in hers. 'You'd better tell me what's happened.'

Lauren took a deep breath. 'I didn't tell my mum and dad I was coming here,' she said.

Serena's mother looked dismayed. 'Oh, Lauren,' she said. 'You shouldn't have done that. Your poor parents will be so worried.'

'I know,' Lauren said.

'Well you'd better ring them up right now and tell them, hadn't you?' Serena's mother picked up the receiver and held it out. Lauren nodded.

'Do you want me to do it for you?'

Lauren shook her head. She knew she had to do it herself, but it was so hard to take the phone and dial the number of her mother's mobile. She hesitated for a moment longer then somehow she managed to make herself do it. The phone at the other end rang just once, then her mother's voice answered.

'Mum, it's me,' Lauren said, and that was all she could say because after that she burst into tears.

Serena's mother took the phone from Lauren. She spoke calmly and patiently to Lauren's parents, giving the address of the house. Then she put the phone down again and turned to Lauren who had stopped crying now, though she was still sniffling. 'You look like you could do with a cup of hot chocolate,' she said.

'Why don't you sit down at the table while I make you one?'

Lauren did as she was told, while Serena's mother put a saucepan of milk on the cooker to heat up and spooned some chocolate powder into a mug.

'What on earth made you do such a silly thing?' she asked while they were waiting for the milk to boil.

'I didn't think they'd let me go if I told them,' Lauren said.

'Is that so?' Serena's mother asked, pouring the hot milk into the mug and stirring in the chocolate. Then she floated a pink marshmallow on the top and put it down in front of Lauren. 'Careful, it's hot!' she said.

The hot chocolate smelled surprisingly good and after she'd had a couple of sips Lauren found she felt a little bit better.

'So why did you think they wouldn't let you come to the party?' Serena's mother asked, sitting down opposite Lauren.

Lauren sighed. 'It's difficult to explain,' she said.

'I'm good at listening to difficult explanations,' Serena's mother told her.

Lauren sipped her chocolate and began trying to explain what had happened. Soon she found she was telling Serena's mother all about how her parents wouldn't let her do things by herself.

'Why do you think that is?' Serena's mother asked.

Lauren took a deep breath. This was something that was very hard to talk about. 'I had a sister called Ruth,' she began. 'She died when she was only two years old.'

'And you think that's got something to do with it?' Serena's mother asked.

'I don't know,' Lauren said. 'Maybe. But just because something terrible happened to Ruth that doesn't mean it's going to happen to me, does it?'

Serena's mother nodded her head slowly. 'But your parents don't know that, do they?' she said. 'Think how worried they must be.'

'I know,' Lauren said. 'But it's still not fair.'

'Never mind,' Serena's mother said. 'If it's any consolation, I know just how you feel.'

'Do you?' asked Lauren. She found it difficult to believe that anyone could know how she felt.

'As a matter of fact I do,' Serena's mother went on. 'You see, when I was young my parents were so strict that I once tried to run away from home.'

'Did you really?' Lauren asked.

'I certainly did.'

'And what happened?'

Serena's mother smiled. 'It started to

pour with rain. I got completely soaked and I came home,' she said. She laughed as she said this and Lauren found herself laughing with her.

'But what happened in the end?' Lauren asked. 'Did your parents stop being so strict or what?'

Serena's mother thought about this for a moment. Then she said, 'In the end I grew up and left home.'

She sounded a little bit sad and Lauren wanted to ask her more, but just then the doorbell rang.

'That'll be your mum and dad,' Serena's mother said. 'Now you just stay calm and tell them you're very, very sorry for what you did and you'll never do it again. Have you got that?'

Lauren nodded.

'And make sure you mean it,' she added, standing up. 'Because if you don't mean it they're never going to believe you.'

CHAPTER NINE

Lauren's mother didn't seem to know whether to hug her daughter or shake her. 'Oh, Lauren!' she said, 'how could you do such a thing to us?'

'I'm sorry, Mum,' Lauren said.

'I thought you were such a sensible girl,' her mother went on, 'but this is one of the most stupid things you could possibly have done. You didn't even leave us an address or a phone number.'

'I won't do it again,' Lauren said. 'I promise.'

'You bet you won't,' her mum told her, 'because I'm never going to let you out of my sight again.'

Lauren listened to this with a sense of dismay.

'Why on earth didn't you tell us about the party?' her mother demanded.

'Because you wouldn't have let me go when you found out it was a sleepover,' Lauren said.

Her mother hesitated and it was her father who spoke next. 'Maybe that's true,' he said quietly.

'It's still no excuse,' her mother said. 'You can't just go somewhere without letting us know where you are. Now come on, we're going home right away.'

Lauren sighed. In a moment she would have to go upstairs, get her coat and bag and tell all the other girls that her parents had arrived to take her home from the party. She could just imagine what Natasha and Sharlene would say. It would be so humiliating. But just then Serena's mother spoke.

'I know we haven't really met,' she told Lauren's parents, 'and maybe it's none of my business, but I did just want to say that I'd very much like Lauren to stay.'

Lauren's parents looked at her in surprise.

'And I'd love you to stay too, just for a chat at least,' she added with a big smile. 'You see we haven't lived here very long and we don't know that many people. That's why we were so keen for Serena to have a party, because it's important to get to know people. So why don't you sit down and have a cup of hot chocolate while you think about it?'

Lauren's mother opened her mouth to reply but she was interrupted by Lauren's father. 'Thanks,' he said. 'That's very nice of you. We'd like that very much.'

Lauren's mother looked as though she was going to object, but in the end she said nothing. They both sat down and Serena's mother began to make more hot chocolate.

As she did so she chatted away to Lauren's parents, asking their advice about the neighbourhood and talking about how different London seemed after living in Barbados. Gradually Lauren noticed that her mother was beginning to look a little less cross. After a while she was even smiling.

Serena's mother put the hot chocolate down on the table in front of Lauren's parents. 'It's so nice the way your daughter and her friends have welcomed my Serena,' she said. 'It hasn't been easy for her, leaving her old friends behind and coming to a strange country, but I must say the girls she's met here have been really lovely.'

Lauren looked at her parents and she could see that they were beginning to soften. After all, how could anyone remain angry while Serena's mother was being so nice to them?

'That's why I wanted Lauren to stay for the rest of the party,' Serena's mother continued. 'I think she's going to be such a good friend for my Serena.'

Lauren looked from her mother to her father and back again. 'Can I?' she said.

Her mother opened her mouth to speak but once again it was her father who got there first. 'Well, I suppose we do know where she is now,' he said.

Lauren wanted to jump in the air and shout hurrah, but she didn't. Instead she looked at her mother, waiting to see what she would say.

Her mother was frowning hard. She looked as though she was trying to make

a very difficult decision. 'Lauren, I want you to promise that you'll never ever do anything like this again,' she said.

'I promise,' Lauren said, and she meant it. She never wanted to have to go through an evening like this again.

Her mother took a deep breath. 'All right then,' she said. 'But you just make sure you keep your promise.'

'Thanks, Mum,' Lauren said. 'And thanks, Dad. And thanks, Mrs Wallington.' Then she turned and ran upstairs as quickly as she could in case they changed their minds.

The other girls were so engrossed in the video they had almost forgotten about Lauren, and she thought at first she might be able to slip back into the room without anyone noticing. But of course Natasha and Sharlene had to know what had been going on. 'Where have you been?' Natasha asked. 'And who was the boy on the phone?'

'Oh it was just a mistake,' Lauren said, finding herself a place to sit down.

'You mean the phone call wasn't for you?' Sharlene asked.

'Well, yes it was.'

'So who was the boy?'

'Just a friend of the family,' Lauren said.

'A friend of the family?'

'Ssh!' Serena told them. 'We're trying to watch the video.'

Natasha and Sharlene exchanged puzzled glances. They would both have liked to know more, but there was nothing else they could discover for the time being, and as far as Lauren was concerned that was the way it was going to stay.

The party was a big success. Everyone enjoyed themselves tremendously. Fortunately, by the time the girls had finished watching videos, Lauren's mother and father had gone home. So she was saved from having to answer questions about why they had come to the house. Serena's mother didn't say anything more about the episode and Lauren was very grateful to her for that. She stayed the night like all the other girls and went home the next morning.

That weekend her mother took her to the shopping mall and they bought a present for Serena, as well as a card and some wrapping paper. The present was a CD of one of Serena's favourite groups and it was quite expensive, but Lauren's mother didn't say a word about that.

Lauren gave the card and the present to Serena on Monday at school, and when Serena opened the present she looked very pleased. Lauren wasn't sure whether Serena's mother had told her what had happened at the party.

If she did know, Serena certainly didn't show it. She said nothing about the phone call and she was just as friendly as before. Lauren didn't mention it either.

Natasha and Sharlene were still curious to know the identity of her mysterious 'boyfriend', but they didn't get any information out of Lauren. She just repeated what she had said at the party. 'It was just an old friend of the family,' she told them.

'But I don't understand why he was phoning up Serena's house,' Natasha said.

'He just wanted to tell me something,' Lauren replied.

'What did he want to tell you that couldn't wait until you got home?' Sharlene demanded.

Lauren raised one eyebrow. 'It's a secret,' she said.

Natasha and Sharlene looked very dissatisfied, but fortunately the bell rang at that moment and they all had to go into class.

'Thanks for the present,' Serena said as they walked into the classroom together.

'That's okay,' Lauren said. 'Thanks for inviting me to your party.'

Serena smiled at her and Lauren had a feeling that they were going to be good friends from now on.

At lunchtime Daniel and Zach were playing football in the playground when Lauren came over to them. They stopped playing and waited for her.

'Hi, Lauren,' Daniel said.

'Hi.'

'What happened after I phoned you up at Serena's party?'

She told him what Serena's mother had said and how her parents had finally agreed to let her stay.

'So it turned out all right in the end?' he said.

'Yeah, because of Serena's mum and because of you too. I wanted to say thanks for phoning me up.'

'That's okay,' Daniel said. 'Actually, the person you should really thank is

Zach. He risked his life for you.'

'Well, not exactly my life,' Zach said, 'but it was a close thing.' Then he told her about hiding under the bed and putting the sticker on Edward's jacket, and they all laughed.

'Did Serena's sister see the sticker?' Lauren asked.

'I don't know,' Zach said. 'Edward didn't say anything about it, but he had a funny look on his face when I saw him the next morning. I thought he was going to say something to me but then he didn't. He hasn't said anything about another date. Maybe you should ask Serena what happened.'

'Maybe I will,' Lauren said.

Of course Natasha and Sharlene weren't satisfied. They kept on asking questions, but Lauren stuck to her story and in the end they gave up.

Daniel was the next one in the class to be nine. He decided he didn't want a party but he got lots of presents. One of them was Zombie Warriors, so he and Zach could play it as much as they liked from that day onwards. He even invited Lauren round to play it and she was pretty good, but then compared to sneaking out of the house and catching a bus to somewhere you've never been before, fighting a horde of killer vampires is a piece of cake.